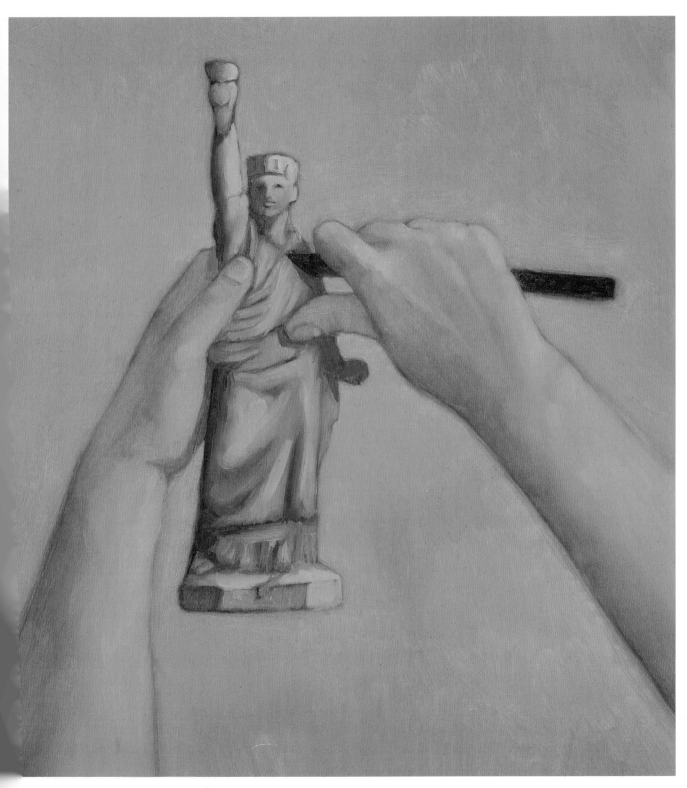

Naming
LIBERTY

Naming
LIBERTY

JANE YOLEN

Paintings by JIM BURKE

PHILOMEL BOOKS

AT THE DINNER TABLE, Papa tells us his big idea.
He looks at Mama serving the bread.
He looks at my brothers—Shmuel, Aron, Jakob—
and at me, Gitl, only seven years old.
Rubbing his beard with a meaty hand, he says,
"I hear we can find a new life across the ocean.
No more pogromists raiding our village,
burning our houses, killing our lambs.
No more generals taking our sons into the army
without even asking our permission.
We must find liberty in the land of America."
Papa's voice throbs like a drum, and is low,
but his voice is always low when he has a big idea.
And this is the biggest.

Versailles, 1865

M. Édouard de Laboulaye had a big idea
at a dinner party in his country house.
He tapped his fork against a glass.
He said that in eleven years,
France's great friend America
would celebrate its hundredth birthday.
"We should build a memorial
to their independence," he said.
"The common work of both our nations."
Everyone at the table applauded—
everyone except one man.
Slim, elegant, with wavy hair and a mustache,
Frédéric Auguste Bartholdi sat thinking:
A monument for America. That was a big idea.

Moving across the ocean
to a brand-new country takes time.
A family cannot move quickly.
So Papa sends Shmuel ahead
to find us a place in America.
"Write to us when you get there,"
Mama says, adjusting Shmuel's cap.
"Write to us when you find work,"
Papa says, patting him on the back.
Aron and Jakob say, "Write to us
about pretty girls and dances and parties."
I whisper, "Just write."

Paris, 1856–1870

Bartholdi was born in 1834 in France.
From the time he was young, he loved art.
His widowed mother, Charlotte, knew
how talented he was, so she sent him to Paris.
There he studied painting and architecture.
But young Bartholdi loved large projects best.
At twenty, traveling in Egypt, he fell under
the spell of the great pyramids and the Sphinx.
He met Count Ferdinand-Marie de Lesseps,
who later built the Suez Canal.
Both young men dreamed large dreams.
But large dreams take time.

Shmuel's letters come every other month.
We read them till they are in shreds.
"In America," he writes in his bold hand,
"I am a greenhorn, someone who is new
to American customs and American ways,
someone who does not have an American name.
So I am calling myself Sammy."
"What is wrong with his old name?" Mama asks.
But I like the name "Sammy."
I like how it bounces on my tongue.
Shmuel who is Sammy has a job now.
He rolls cigars in a factory where
people are paid to read newspapers aloud
to the workers, in Yiddish and English.
This helps him learn to speak like an American.

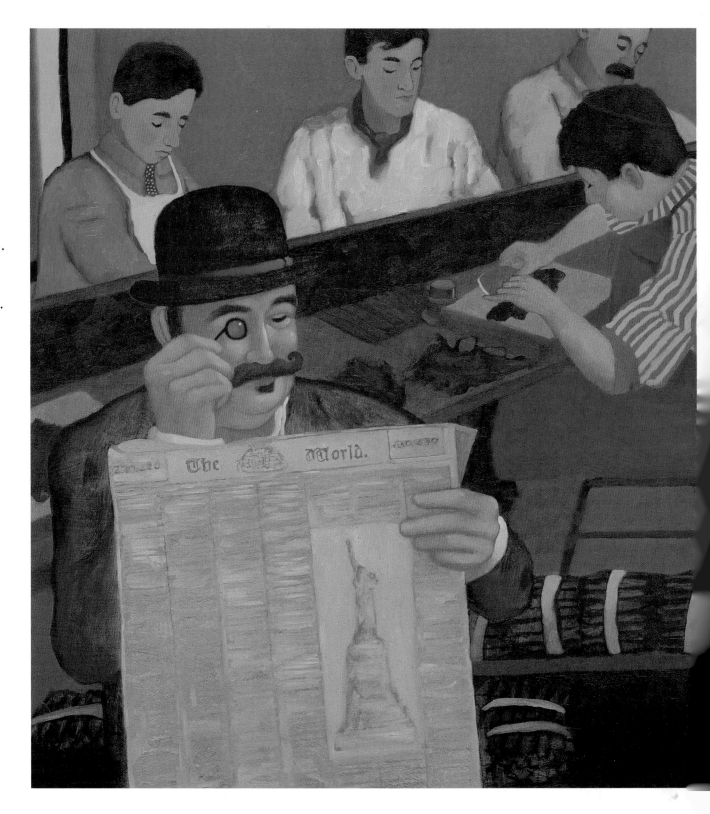

Alsace, 1870–1871

It took a war to stop Bartholdi
from working on his great statue.
In 1870, Germany invaded France
and Bartholdi hurried home to Alsace,
the part of France where he'd been born.
There, Germans occupied his mother's home.
He was made captain of the French troops.
When he had to surrender his town,
he wept alone in his room.
But a year later, the French prevailed.
Now Bartholdi knew firsthand
how precious freedom was.
At last he sailed to America
to talk about his monument to freedom.

It takes two years of Shmuel's letters,
sometimes with copper coins packed inside,
before we are ready to join him in America.
We have to sell our dairy cows and chickens.
We have to sell our ewes and lambs.
We find a new home for the cat.
Our plowhorse, Simcha, is sold,
along with the farmhouse and farm.
Mama cries as she packs the dishes
into wooden crates, our clothes into valises.
Aron and Jakob snuffle good-bye to their friends.
Even Papa wipes a tear saying farewell to Simcha.
I seem to be the only one excited to sail the ocean
to find liberty and a new American name.

On the road, 1871–1872

Bartholdi's ship sailed into New York Harbor
where Bedloe's Island stood.
Bartholdi was full of excitement. He said,
"Here my statue to freedom must rise."
In his mind he gave the island a new name.
He called it Liberty Island.
It would be an immigrant's first view
of America's promised liberty.
Then Bartholdi traveled from city to city,
speaking to many prominent Americans—
even to President Ulysses S. Grant—
trying to excite them all about his idea.
But it is a long way from an idea
to making a monument for freedom.

Shmuel arranges with a steamship company
for tickets on a boat bound for America.
But we live many miles from the ocean,
and many more miles from America.
We sit at the dinner table and I ask,
"How do we get from here to there?"
Papa laughs, his blue eyes twinkling.
"By cart," Aron says, punching my shoulder.
"By foot," says Jakob, pulling my braids.
"By train," Mama says, hand over her heart.
"By all of these," says Papa, "with God's help."
And with God's help, I think,
I will find a new name.

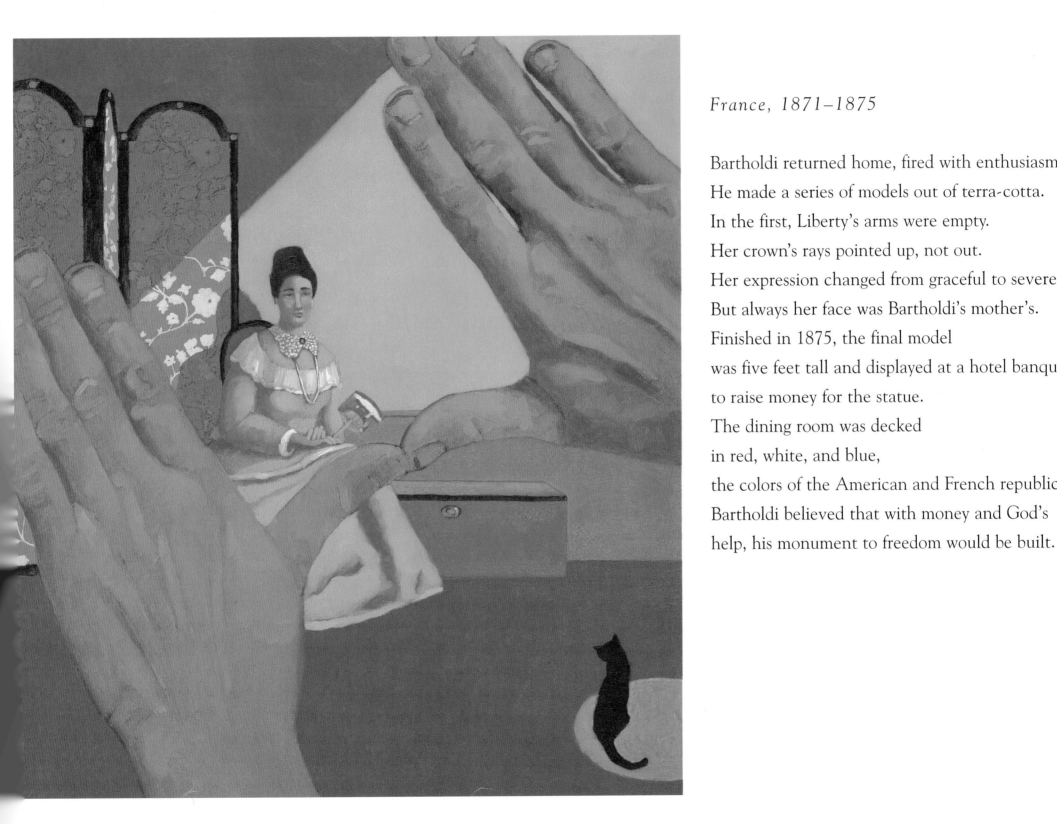

France, 1871–1875

Bartholdi returned home, fired with enthusiasm.
He made a series of models out of terra-cotta.
In the first, Liberty's arms were empty.
Her crown's rays pointed up, not out.
Her expression changed from graceful to severe.
But always her face was Bartholdi's mother's.
Finished in 1875, the final model
was five feet tall and displayed at a hotel banquet
to raise money for the statue.
The dining room was decked
in red, white, and blue,
the colors of the American and French republics.
Bartholdi believed that with money and God's
help, his monument to freedom would be built.

Mama sews coins into our coat linings
so that no one can steal our money.
Then Butcher Kalman loads us onto his cart
with our three crates and four valises.
At a smelly hotel in Kiev we meet an agent.
He speaks Russian and Ukrainian and Yiddish.
Unsmiling, he tells us we have to wait.
"I miss Yekaterinoslaf already," Mama says.
Ten other families are at the hotel,
some with bundles tied up with string,
some wearing layers of clothing,
afraid a valise might be stolen away.
I remember our gray cat,
and for the first time, I am a little sad.

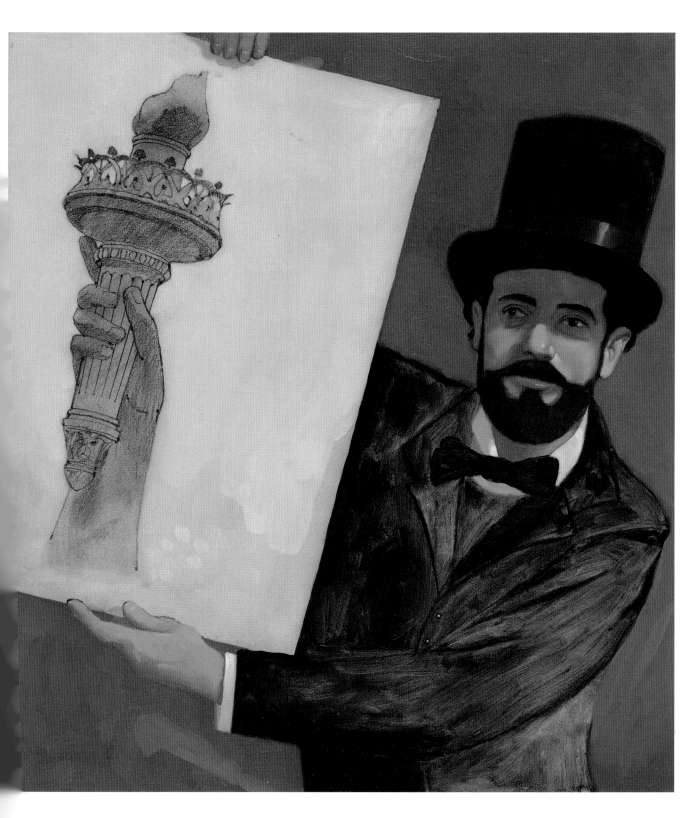

The banquet at the Hotel du Louvre
raised a starting sum—40,000 francs.
By year's end contributors in France
had added more: 200,000 francs in all.
Bartholdi was relieved. He had the passion,
but now the hard work could begin.
He met with many craftsmen—
plasterers, carpenters, metalworkers.
He showed them his models and drawings.
The craftsmen would start by making
Liberty's right hand holding a torch.
Though the whole statue would not be ready
for the American centennial,
Bartholdi was not sad.

It is many days till the right train comes.

Each day we go to the station and wait.

Papa smokes with the men,

Mama chats with the women.

Aron and Jakob tease the girls,

smiling at them and telling lies.

But I run up and down the station,

turning around till my skirts bell out.

The rubles in the lining of my coat

bang against my legs.

I am so excited, I cannot settle down.

I want to be an American, to have a new name.

But it is a long way from here to our liberty.

Paris and Philadelphia, 1876

Bartholdi's monumental statue
was made in sections of copper
because copper was easy to work with
and was lighter and cheaper than brass.
Bartholdi always had to think of the expense.
It took twenty craftsmen working
ten hours every day for half a year
to finish the hand and torch in time
for the Philadelphia Exposition.
By June 1876, a full month
after the Exposition opened,
the thirty-foot section was ready.
In August it was shipped from Paris,
a long way over the ocean to Philadelphia.

At last our train chugs into the station,
its steam rising around us like great clouds.
The unsmiling agent hurries us up the steps.
We crowd in with boxes, crates, bags, tins.
Then the train starts up, creaking, groaning,
like an old woman getting out of bed.
Sitting next to Mama, I watch as we cross
Europe. The countryside speeds by.
"Faster! Faster!" I pray, for the faster we go,
the sooner we will be in America, and
the sooner I will have an American name.

America, 1876–1877

Bartholdi crossed America many times
raising money, asking for support.
On February 22, 1877, Congress voted
to accept the statue as a gift from France.
They voted as well to maintain the statue
and to find a site on which it could stand.
They found an architect to make a pedestal.
Bartholdi decided to call his statue
Liberty Enlightening the World.
It was a big name for a big statue,
but it was not her American name.

Days go by, fast and slow.
We eat and sleep on the train.
Then the train stops in a big field
with a single house squatting in the middle.
"Out! Out!" cries the agent, herding us
as if we are sheep into the house.
Inside are white-clad men and women
Who—like angry angels—take our clothes
and boil them in kettles on the stove.
We are thrust into showers.
The agent says, "If you are dirty or sick,
you cannot get on the boat to America."
So we endure it all—the fear, the steam,
the showers, the confusion.

Paris, 1878

Liberty's head was built next.
It took more than a year.
Many metalworkers put it together
under Bartholdi's steady gaze.
In June 1878, the head was moved
from the workshop
to the Paris Universal Exposition.
It went through the streets of Paris
on a huge cart drawn by heavy horses.
People lined the dawn streets,
a boil of bodies, a great confusion,
to watch the massive head rocking
with the motion of the cart.
Liberty seemed to nod at the onlookers.

At last we come to the city of Bremen,
where a boat is waiting for us.
It is small, filthy, packed with people.
All we have left to eat is herring and bread,
which Mama has kept in her carryall.
We spend over twenty days on the boat.
There are two tiers of bunks
in the dark, smelly hold
reached by climbing down narrow stairs.
At night it is hard to sleep
because people snore around us, above us;
because of the low, sad sound of the foghorn.
But I pretend the foghorn is saying,
"Soon you will be free in America."

Paris, 1881–1884

Now it was time to build Liberty's body.
First Bartholdi had to find an engineer
who understood how to make a structure
strong enough to hold thirty-two tons of copper.
He turned to Alexandre-Gustave Eiffel,
known as "The Magician of Iron."
Agreeing to design Liberty's inside,
Eiffel put a double spiral staircase in her body.
Inside she was clean and empty but for the stairs.
A photo taken on July 4, 1884, in Paris
showed Bartholdi at the foot of Liberty
as he presented her to his fellow citizens.
She towered over the Paris rooftops.
Soon she would be sent to America.

It is so hot in the hold, too hot.

I go on deck to breathe in the ocean air.

The agent is clinging to the rail,

staring out across the water.

"Are you a greenhorn, sir?" I ask.

For the first time, he smiles.

"No, child. I am an agent."

"Then you have an American name?"

He laughs. "In the old country

I am called Velvul."

I nod. I know the name. It means "Wolf."

"But here in America, I am called Will."

I say his name softly, a kind of prayer,

that I, too, shall find an American name.

America, Paris, and Rouen, 1884–1885

American Richard Morris Hunt designed
the pedestal, his expensive plan reworked
several times.
Newspaper owner Joseph Pulitzer helped raise
the extra money.
July 4, 1884, though still in France,
the statue was officially given to America.
Bartholdi took guests into her body,
leading them up and down the spiral stairs.
The following year, Liberty was dismantled
and packed into 214 crates.
A train of seventy cars carried her to Rouen.
After a month on the ocean, she arrived in
New York, where she was greeted
by a huge number of ships.
Some 10,000 people on the ships and shore
cheered and waved handkerchiefs and flags.

We sail into a harbor
where a huge shining statue of a woman
holds up a lamp to welcome us in.
"That is Lady Liberty," Will tells me.
"She came here in crates, by train, then boat."
"Just like me," I say, and he grins.
A white bird flies overhead.
Around us people come onto the deck,
shouting, pointing, waving, cheering.
Aron and Jakob throw their caps in the air.
Suddenly I ask: "Is Liberty an American name?"
Will nods. "Very American," he tells me.

New York, October 28, 1886

The pedestal was completed in April.
By October 25, Liberty was reassembled.
She was 151 feet high from the top of her base
to the tip of her flaming torch.
She was 305 feet high if the foundation
and pedestal were counted.
Dedication Day dawned gray and rainy. Liberty's
face was veiled with a French flag.
Ecstatic, Bartholdi pulled a special cord,
and the flag on Liberty's face came off.
Standing tall on the island,
she gazed out over the harbor.
A gift from France, she was now an American.

We get off the boat at Ellis Island,

where people ask us many questions.

A doctor checks us all over.

Then a man writes my name

on a landing card and hands it to me.

But it is my old name—Gitl. I feel like crying.

I turn and see Shmuel—Sammy—waiting.

I almost don't recognize him.

Then I run and jump into his arms.

"Welcome to America, Gitl," he says.

I realize then that I am no greenhorn.

"Here in America," I say, "my name is Liberty.

But you can call me Libby."

And he does.

New York, October 28, 1886

Twenty-one years after de Laboulaye's big idea,
Lady Liberty was welcomed to America.
In the harbor navy ships ferried special guests
over to Bedloe's Island for the ceremony.
The only females allowed there
were Bartholdi's wife, Jeanne-Emile, and
de Lesseps' eight-year-old daughter, Tototte.
The man-of-war guns sounded,
small boats blew their steam whistles,
and thousands of people cheered.
Bartholdi would later say of that day,
about his long passion for the statue,
"The dream of my life is accomplished."
And it was.

What is true about this book

The story of Libby's journey combines the immigration stories of my mother's and father's families. My father's family (the Yolens) came from Yekaterinoslaf in the Ukraine, not steerage but second class because my grandfather was a bottler and had a bit of money. Their oldest son had been sent ahead to make way for the rest. My father was a four-year-old named Velvul— Wolf—always known in America as Will. My mother's father's family (the Berlins) came from Ligum in Lithuania, where they were dairy farmers. The father and three oldest boys came first and worked in a cigar-rolling factory.

I also found details of the immigrant journey in some of the following books: Sholom Aleichem's *Adventures of Mottel, the Cantor's Son*, New York: Henry Schuman, 1905, 1953; Irving Howe's *World of Our Fathers: The Journey of the East European Jews to America and the Life They Found and Made*, New York: Schocken Books, 1976, 1989; Ellen Levine's *If Your Name Was Changed at Ellis Island*, New York: Scholastic Inc., 1993; Milton Meltzer's *The Jewish Americans: A History in Their Own Words, 1650–1950*, New York: Thomas Y. Crowell, 1982; Milton Meltzer's *World of Our Fathers: The Jews of Eastern Europe*, New York: Farrar, Straus and Giroux, 1974; Joachim Neugroschel's *The Shtetl: A Creative Anthology of Jewish Life in Eastern Europe*, New York: Perigee Books/ G. P. Putnam's Sons, 1979; Diane and David Roskies' *The Shtetl Book*, Ktav Publishing House, Inc., 1975, 1979; and Ronald Sanders' *Shores of Refuge: A Hundred Years of Jewish Emigration*, New York: Henry Holt and Company, 1988.

The story of Liberty's journey is well documented. The statue is located on what was known as Bedloe's Island until 1956, when it was legally renamed Liberty Island, which is how Bartholdi had always thought of it. The island is slightly southwest of the southern tip of Manhattan. Open to visitors who arrive by ferry, the statue has a viewing area in its crown that provides a broad panorama of the harbor. While Liberty is Bartholdi's most famous work, critics believe his masterpiece is a statue known as *The Lion of Belfort*. Made of red sandstone, this colossal lion is carved in the side of a mountain overlooking the town of Belfort. It is one of a number of patriotic sculptures Bartholdi made that were inspired by the town's struggle against the German assault in the Franco-Prussian War. Bartholdi also produced a huge range of other works of art, including bas-reliefs, medallions, busts, fountains, and tombs.

Liberty is not a simple statue. Her crown has seven rays of light for the seven continents (Europe, North America, Asia, Africa, Australia, Antarctica, and South America). It also represents her reign as queen of liberty. In her left hand, she holds a book of law on which in Roman numerals is the date of America's independence. Liberty's right hand clutches a torch, a flame of hope, a beacon to sailors. As the Emma Lazarus poem at the statue's base ends, "Send these, the homeless, tempest-tost to me, / I lift my lamp beside the golden door!"

Among the many books and articles I consulted were: Sue Burchard's *The Statue of Liberty: Birth to Rebirth*, New York: Harcourt Brace Jovanovich, 1985; Lynn Curlee's *Liberty*, New York: Aladdin Paperbacks, 2003; Alice J. Hall's "Liberty Lifts Her Lamps Once More," *National Geographic*, 1986; and websites including
http://www.corrosion-doctors.org/Landmarks/statue-sculptor.htm
http://www.cr.nps.gov/history/online_books/hh/11/hh11l.htm

Jane Yolen

For Pat Gauch, who always gives me liberty in my projects.   —J.Y.

Like Bartholdi, I too have been blessed with a wonderful, loving mother
who has always been an amazing inspiration in my life, and in my art. I love you, Mom.   —J.B.

When Liberty was constructed, her contours were sharply stated in rich salmon with shades of orange and deep browns—the colors of copper. Through natural weathering and oxidation, Liberty's copper changed from salmon to browns, then grays, to the well-known patina color—greenish aqua. The weathering of copper in seacoast settings generally takes from five to seven years. To represent the transforming palette of Liberty, the paintings were created on rich orange/brownish (burnt sienna) oil-washed boards, with the familiar aqua patina color spread generously throughout many of the compositions. —J.B.

Patricia Lee Gauch, Editor

PHILOMEL BOOKS
A division of Penguin Young Readers Group.   Published by The Penguin Group.
Penguin Group (USA) Inc., 375 Hudson Street, New York, NY 10014, U.S.A.
Penguin Group (Canada), 90 Eglinton Avenue East, Suite 700, Toronto, Ontario M4P 2Y3, Canada (a division of Pearson Penguin Canada Inc.).
Penguin Books Ltd, 80 Strand, London WC2R 0RL, England.
Penguin Ireland, 25 St. Stephen's Green, Dublin 2, Ireland (a division of Penguin Books Ltd).
Penguin Group (Australia), 250 Camberwell Road, Camberwell, Victoria 3124, Australia (a division of Pearson Australia Group Pty Ltd).
Penguin Books India Pvt Ltd, 11 Community Centre, Panchsheel Park, New Delhi - 110 017, India.
Penguin Group (NZ), 67 Apollo Drive, Rosedale, North Shore 0632, New Zealand (a division of Pearson New Zealand Ltd).
Penguin Books (South Africa) (Pty) Ltd, 24 Sturdee Avenue, Rosebank, Johannesburg 2196, South Africa.
Penguin Books Ltd, Registered Offices: 80 Strand, London WC2R 0RL, England.

Design by Semadar Megged.   Text set in 13-point Goudy Old Style.   The paintings for this book were created in oil on gessoed bristol board.

Library of Congress Cataloging-in-Publication Data
Yolen, Jane.   Naming Liberty / by Jane Yolen ; illustrated by Jim Burke.   p. cm.   Summary: In parallel stories, a Ukrainian Jewish family prepares to emigrate to the United States in the late 1800s, and Frédéric Auguste Bartholdi designs, raises funds for, and builds the Statue of Liberty in honor of the United States' centennial.   [1. Emigration and immigration—Fiction. 2. Jews—Fiction. 3. Bartholdi, Frédéric Auguste, 1834–1904—Fiction. 4. Statue of Liberty (New York, N.Y.)—Fiction. 5. United States—History—1865–1898—Fiction.] I. Burke, Jim, ill. II. Title.   PZ7.Y78Nam 2008   [Fic]—dc22   2007038636
ISBN 978-0-399-24250-2
1 3 5 7 9 10 8 6 4 2